A GOLDEN BOOK • NEW YORK

www.goldenbooks.com
www.randomhouse.com/kids/disney
Library of Congress Control Number: 2008928536
ISBN: 978-0-7364-2567-4
MANUFACTURED IN SINGAPORE
10 9 8 7 6 5 4 3 2 1

King Triton, the great sea king, had many daughters who loved the undersea world.

But Triton's youngest daughter, Ariel, dreamed of the world above the water's surface—the world of humans.

Ariel and her friend Flounder liked to go to the surface to visit Scuttle the seagull. Scuttle told them all about the humans' objects that Ariel found at the bottom of the sea.

One day Triton learned about Ariel's trips to the surface. The sea king grew very angry. He asked his friend Sebastian the crab to keep an eye on Ariel.

A few days later, Ariel noticed a ship sailing way up on the surface of the water. She quickly swam toward it.

"Ariel! Ariel! Please come back!" cried Sebastian as he and Flounder swam after her.

When Ariel surfaced, she saw a huge ship filled with sailors. Ariel's eyes lit up when she spotted the sailor the others called Prince Eric. It was love at first sight!

Suddenly the sky darkened. Heavy rain began to fall, and lightning split the sky. The ship was tossed on the waves, and the prince was thrown overboard!

"I've got to save him!" thought Ariel. She grabbed the drowning prince and swam to shore, pulling him onto the beach. Prince Eric did not stir as Ariel gently touched his face and sang him a love song.

Soon Ariel heard the prince's crew searching for him. She did not want to be seen by the humans, so she kissed the prince and dove back into the sea.

Prince Eric awoke to find Sir Grimsby, his loyal steward, at his side. Sir Grimsby was happy that Eric was alive.

"A girl . . . rescued me," said the prince. "She was singing. She had the most beautiful voice."

Prince Eric, too, had fallen in love.

King Triton was furious when he discovered that Ariel had fallen in love with a human. He rushed to the grotto where Ariel kept her collection of humans' treasures.

"Contact between the human world and the merworld is strictly forbidden!" Triton shouted.

He raised his magic trident and fired bolts of energy around the cave, destroying the treasures. Then the mighty sea king left.

Ariel buried her face in her hands and began to cry.

Meanwhile, not far away, evil forces were at work in the undersea kingdom. Ursula, the sea witch, who had tried once before to overthrow Triton, was looking for a way to take over. Through her crystal ball she could see Ariel crying, and an idea came to her.

Ursula sent her slimy eel servants, Flotsam and Jetsam, to Ariel's grotto. There they convinced the Little Mermaid that Ursula could help her to get her beloved prince. Ariel was so upset that she ignored Sebastian's warnings and swam off with Flotsam and Jetsam to meet with the sea witch.

"My dear," said the witch. "Here's the deal. I'll make a potion that will turn you into a human for three days. Before the sun sets on the third day, you've got to get dear old princie to kiss you. If he kisses you, you'll remain human permanently. But if he doesn't, you turn back into a mermaid and you belong to me!"

In return for the potion, the witch wanted Ariel's voice.

"My voice?" asked Ariel. "Without my voice, how can I—"

"You'll still have your looks, your pretty face," replied Ursula.

After Ariel agreed to Ursula's deal, an amazing change took place. Ariel's voice flew from her body and was captured in a seashell around Ursula's neck. Ariel lost her tail, grew legs, and became a human.

When Ariel went in search of the prince, she was helped ashore by her friends. She tried to speak to them, but no sound came out.

A short while later, Ariel saw Prince Eric. The prince had been lovesick ever since hearing her sing. At first the prince thought Ariel was the girl who had rescued him. But when he learned that she couldn't speak, he knew he was wrong.

Prince Eric felt sorry for Ariel. She needed a place to stay, so he took her back to his palace.

Over the next two days, Prince Eric grew to like
Ariel more and more. During a romantic boat ride,
Eric was about to kiss Ariel when Flotsam and Jetsam
overturned the boat.

"That was a close one. Too close," said Ursula, who
was watching in her crystal ball. "It's time Ursula took
matters into her own tentacles." The sea witch mixed
a magic potion and changed herself into a beautiful
young maiden.

On the morning of the third day, there was great excitement throughout the kingdom. Prince Eric was going to marry a young maiden he had just met!

Ursula, disguised as the maiden, had used Ariel's voice to trick Eric. He now believed that the maiden was the girl who had saved him from the shipwreck.

Poor Ariel was heartbroken.

The wedding ceremony was to take place on Prince Eric's new boat. Scuttle flew by just as the bride passed in front of a mirror. Her reflection was that of the sea witch! Scuttle rushed off to tell Ariel and the rest of his friends.

Sebastian quickly formed a plan. Flounder helped Ariel get out to Eric's ship. Scuttle arranged for some of his seagull friends to delay the wedding. And Sebastian hurried to find King Triton.

Prince Eric and the maiden were about to be married when a flock of seagulls, led by Scuttle, swooped down on the bride. She screamed in the sea witch's voice.

Scuttle knocked the seashell containing Ariel's voice from around the maiden's neck. The shell shattered, and Ariel's voice returned to her.

"It was you all the time!" said Prince Eric.

"Oh, Eric, I wanted to tell you," said Ariel.

The sun disappeared over the horizon just as they were about to kiss. Ariel's three days were up. She changed back into a mermaid. Ursula grabbed Ariel and dove off the ship.

Thanks to Sebastian's warning, Triton was waiting for them at Ursula's lair. "I might be willing to make an exchange for someone better," cried Ursula. Triton agreed, and he became Ursula's prisoner. She now had his magic trident and control of the undersea kingdom.

All of a sudden a harpoon struck Ursula in the shoulder. Prince Eric had come to Ariel's rescue! Together they swam to the surface.

Ursula followed close behind them, and she grew
bigger and bigger with anger, until she rose out of the
water.

Prince Eric swam to his ship and climbed on board.
He grabbed the wheel and turned the ship toward
Ursula. Just as the sea witch was about to fire a deadly
bolt at Ariel from the trident, the prince's ship
slammed into Ursula. The evil witch was destroyed!

Now that the witch was gone, Triton was freed. He rose from the sea and saw Ariel watching Prince Eric, who was lying on the shore, unconscious.

"She really does love him, doesn't she?" asked the sea king.

Sebastian, who was nearby, nodded.

"I'm going to miss her," Triton added. Then he raised his trident and shot a magic bolt at Ariel's tail.

The Little Mermaid's tail disappeared, and once again she had legs. Ariel was now a human. Prince Eric awoke in time to see his beloved Ariel running onto the shore. He kissed her, and they were married that day. After the wedding, Prince Eric and Ariel sailed off on their honeymoon to live happily ever after.

Beauty and the Beast

Once upon a time there lived a young prince in a beautiful castle. Although he had everything his heart desired, the prince was spoiled and selfish.

One winter's night, an old beggar woman asked the prince for shelter from the cold. In return she offered him a rose. Repulsed by the old woman, the unkind prince turned her away.

The woman warned him not to be deceived by appearances, since beauty is found within. When the prince dismissed her again, the old woman's ugliness melted away to reveal a beautiful enchantress.

The prince tried to apologize, but it was too late. The enchantress knew there was no love in his heart.

As punishment, the enchantress turned the prince into a hideous beast. Then she placed a spell on the castle and all who lived there.

The rose she had offered him was an enchanted rose. It would bloom until the prince was twenty-one. If he could learn to love and be loved in return before the last petal fell, then the spell would be broken. If not, he would remain a beast forever.

Ashamed of his monstrous form, the Beast hid inside the castle. A magic mirror was his only window to the outside world.

As the years passed, he fell into despair. Slowly the rose began to wither. He did not believe anyone could ever love him.

In a nearby village there lived a beautiful young woman named Belle. Belle, unlike the other girls in the village, cared only for her books. She always felt out of place.

Belle loved to read about adventure and romance. Her father, Maurice, loved books, too. Maurice was an inventor—a genius, according to Belle; a crackpot, according to the townsfolk.

"Belle is even stranger than her father," the villagers whispered. "Her nose is always in a book, and her head is in the clouds."

Gaston, the handsomest man in town, wanted to make Belle his wife. Even though she thought he was a brainless brute and turned him down again and again, Gaston was determined to wed the lovely Belle.

One cold day Maurice hitched his horse, Phillipe, to a wagon and set off to show his latest invention at a faraway fair.

But Maurice read the map wrong and became lost in a forest. As an icy wind whistled through the trees, he suddenly heard the howling of wolves! Phillipe bolted, and Maurice fell to the ground. Trying to escape the wolves, the frightened man ran deeper and deeper into the woods.

He came to a castle and stumbled inside. There he
was greeted by Mrs. Potts the teapot, Cogsworth the
clock, and Lumiere the candelabrum, who had all been
servants to the prince. But before he had time to marvel
over these strange creatures, an even stranger one
appeared—the Beast!

When Maurice stared in horror, the Beast howled
angrily. Then he scooped Maurice up and carried him
off to a dungeon.

Meanwhile, Phillipe had made his way back home. Belle took one look at the riderless horse and knew something awful had happened to her father.

"Phillipe! Take me to him!" she cried, leaping into the horse's saddle. Without a pause, Phillipe thundered off toward the woods.

When they reached the castle, Belle burst inside and
searched frantically for her father. The enchanted
objects led her to the dungeon, but just as she found
Maurice, the Beast appeared. Belle let out a terrified
gasp at the sight of the hideous creature.

She begged the Beast to free her father. When he
refused, she bravely offered to take Maurice's place.

"No, Belle!" Maurice cried, but the Beast agreed to
the exchange.

Before Belle could bid her father good-bye, the Beast
led her to her room. "The castle is now your home," he
said gruffly. Belle was free to go anywhere she liked—
except the West Wing.

"You will join me for dinner," the Beast ordered.
"That's not a request."

Still, Belle refused, and the Beast stomped off in anger.

That night Belle slipped out of her room and found her way to the forbidden West Wing.

There she saw the enchanted rose by the window. When she reached out to touch it, the Beast suddenly appeared on the balcony outside the window.

Belle screamed and fled from the room.

Her heart pounding, Belle ran out of the castle, mounted Phillipe, and galloped off into the night. But a pack of wolves soon had them surrounded. Belle was helpless.

Suddenly the Beast was there, throwing the wolves aside. Belle heard terrible snarling and howling as the Beast and the wolves battled for their lives. At last the wolves ran off into the woods, but the Beast lay in the snow, badly injured.

Back at the castle, Belle carefully tended to the Beast's wounds. Gentle as she was, the Beast roared in agony.

"I barely touched you," said Belle. Then she saw the look of pain on his face. "I forgot to thank you for saving my life," she added softly.

The Beast only grunted in reply. But when Belle turned away, a hint of a smile appeared on his face.

In the days that followed, the Beast tried to be a proper
host. He showed Belle his library, and she began to teach
him how to act like a gentleman.

"Perhaps it isn't too late," Cogsworth whispered to Mrs.
Potts and her son, Chip the teacup. "If Belle could only love
the Beast, this dreadful spell might yet be broken."

Before long, Belle thought of the Beast as her dearest friend. And the Beast thought of little but the beautiful Belle.

One night while she was teaching him to dance, the Beast asked, "Belle, are you happy here—with me?"

"Yes," she said without hesitation. But the Beast saw a trace of sadness in her eyes. Then Belle added, "If only I could see my father again, even for a minute."

"You can," the Beast said, handing her the magic mirror.

Belle gazed into it and saw Maurice trudging through the forest. He looked frail and old. As she watched, he collapsed in a heap.

"I must go to him!" Belle cried. "He might be dying!"

"I release you," the Beast said sadly. "But take the mirror. Then you will always have a way to look back and remember me."

   With the magic mirror to guide her, Belle soon found
her father and brought him home. But their happy
reunion was cut short by a pounding on their cottage
door. The townspeople had come to take Maurice away.
   Gaston's friend LeFou stepped forward. "Maurice has
been raving that you were imprisoned by a hideous beast,"
he said. "Only a crazy man would tell such a tale."

"But it's true," Belle protested. Her worried eyes searched the angry crowd and fell on Gaston. "Gaston!" she cried. "You know my father isn't crazy. Tell them."

Gaston whispered to Belle that he might be able to calm the crowd—if she promised to marry him.

"Never!" Belle exclaimed. "And my father is not crazy. There really is a beast, and I can prove it." She turned to the crowd. "Look in this mirror and see."

The townspeople looked at the Beast in the magic mirror and grew frightened.

"We must hunt down this savage animal!" Gaston cried.

After locking Belle and her father in the cellar of the cottage, the villagers rode off to storm the Beast's castle.

Luckily, little Chip had stowed away in Belle's saddlebag. After the villagers were gone, he used Maurice's latest invention to release Belle and Maurice from the cellar.

By the time Belle reached the castle, the townspeople had broken in. Gaston and the Beast were fighting on the castle roof. The Beast managed to knock Gaston's weapon from his hand. There was nothing to stop him from killing Gaston.

Gaston screamed for mercy, and the Beast turned away from his enemy. Then Belle watched helplessly as Gaston plunged a knife into the Beast's back.

The Beast roared in pain. Backing away from the wounded Beast, Gaston lost his footing and fell off the roof into the fog below.

Belle rushed to the Beast's side.

"You came back," the Beast said weakly. "At least I can see you one last time."

"No! No!" Belle said, sobbing as she kissed his cheek. "Please don't die. . . . I love you."

At that moment the spell was broken. In one magical instant, the Beast turned back into a prince, and the enchanted servants returned to their human forms.

The castle came to life with rejoicing. There was no doubt that the loving couple would live happily ever after.

One night, an evil man named Jafar and his wicked
parrot, Iago, were waiting in a faraway desert.

Soon a thief named Gazeem rode up to them and
held out the missing half of a scarab medallion. When
Jafar fit the halves together, lightning flashed and the
medallion raced across the sand.

Jafar and the thief followed the medallion to the
Cave of Wonders. Jafar ordered Gazeem to get the
magic lamp that was hidden inside. But when the thief
entered, he was eaten by the tiger head entrance!

Then the tiger head spoke: "Only one who is worthy
may enter here!"

The next morning, a poor young man named Aladdin and his monkey, Abu, were walking through the marketplace of Agrabah. Suddenly Aladdin noticed a pretty young woman. It was love at first sight!

The young woman took an apple from a fruit seller's cart to give to a hungry boy. When the man demanded payment, which she did not have, Aladdin and Abu rushed to help her.

"Thank you for finding my sister," Aladdin said to the fruit seller. He quickly led the young woman away.

"This is your first time in the marketplace, huh?" asked Aladdin.

"I ran away," the young woman explained. "My father is forcing me to get married."

Suddenly, palace guards appeared. They arrested Aladdin under orders from Jafar, the Sultan's advisor. The young woman demanded that they release him. She was really Princess Jasmine, the Sultan's daughter!

Princess Jasmine returned to the palace and ordered Jafar to release Aladdin. Jafar told her it was too late—the young man had been killed.

But Aladdin was not dead. Jafar had learned that Aladdin was the only person worthy to enter the Cave of Wonders. Aladdin could bring the magic lamp to Jafar!

Jafar took Aladdin to the Cave of Wonders. "Proceed," said the tiger head. "Touch nothing but the lamp."

Aladdin and Abu gasped when they saw all the gold and jewels in the cavern. They even found a Magic Carpet!

But just as Aladdin spotted the magic lamp, Abu touched a huge, glittering jewel.

With a loud rumble, the cave began to collapse. Aladdin and Abu were trapped!

But Abu still had the magic lamp!
Aladdin took the old lamp and tried to rub off some of the dust.
Poof! In a flash of swirling smoke, a gigantic genie appeared.
"You're a lot smaller than my last master," he said to Aladdin.

The Genie whisked them all out of the cave on the Magic
Carpet. Then he told Aladdin that he had three wishes.

Aladdin asked the Genie what *he* would wish for.

The Genie replied, "I would wish for freedom!"

So Aladdin promised to use his third wish to set the Genie
free. But his *first* wish was to be a prince—so that he could
marry Princess Jasmine.

Meanwhile, at the palace, Jafar used his serpent staff to hypnotize the Sultan. The poor Sultan was about to agree that Jafar could marry Jasmine.

Suddenly they heard the sounds of a parade. The spell was broken. The Sultan rushed to the balcony in time to see the arrival of a grand prince. It was Aladdin!

Aladdin entered the throne room.

"Your Majesty," he said, bowing to the Sultan. "I am Prince Ali Ababwa. I have come to seek your daughter's hand in marriage."

The Sultan was thrilled! The law stated that Jasmine must marry a prince before her next birthday—which was only days away.

But the princess did not want to marry Prince Ali. She was not in love with him.

Prince Ali offered the princess a ride on his Magic Carpet, hoping to win her love.

During the magical journey, Princess Jasmine realized that Prince Ali was the young man who had helped her in the marketplace. That starry night, Aladdin and Princess Jasmine fell in love.

Jafar didn't want anyone else to marry Jasmine and foil his evil plans. He was so angry that he had Prince Ali captured and thrown into the sea.

Luckily, Aladdin had the magic lamp with him. He summoned the Genie and asked for his second wish— to save his life! The Genie quickly transported Aladdin back to the palace in Agrabah.

Jafar was determined to marry Princess Jasmine.

"I will never marry you, Jafar!" cried Jasmine. "I choose Prince Ali!"

But the Sultan was under Jafar's spell, and he ordered his daughter to marry Jafar.

Suddenly, Aladdin burst into the throne room and smashed Jafar's serpent staff.

"He's been controlling you with this, Your Highness!" said Aladdin.

Immediately, the spell was broken.

"Traitor!" shouted the Sultan. "Guards, arrest Jafar!"

But before they could capture him, Jafar escaped to his secret laboratory.

As Jafar fled, he noticed that Prince Ali was carrying the magic lamp. The prince was really Aladdin! Jafar ordered his parrot to steal the lamp.

When Iago returned, Jafar made the Genie appear. "I wish to be Sultan!" he demanded.

The moment had come for the Sultan to announce the wedding of Princess Jasmine and Prince Ali Ababwa. A cheering crowd had gathered in front of the palace.

Suddenly Jafar appeared—in the Sultan's robes! The crowd gasped.

"Genie, what have you done?" Aladdin shouted.

"Sorry, kid," said the Genie sadly. "I've got a new master now."

Then Jafar made his second wish—to be the most powerful sorcerer in the world. Jafar the sorcerer lost no time turning Prince Ali back into Aladdin.

"Jasmine, I'm sorry!" cried Aladdin. "I'm not a prince. I can't marry you."

Finally Jafar banished Aladdin to the ends of the earth. When Aladdin found himself a million miles from nowhere, he was glad that Abu and the Magic Carpet were still with him. "Back to Agrabah!" he shouted to the Carpet. "As fast as you can!"

Jafar was in the throne room, enjoying his newfound power, when Aladdin appeared. "How many times do I have to destroy you, boy?" he roared.

"You cowardly snake!" Aladdin shouted.

"Snake?" snarled Jafar. With a loud hiss, he turned himself into a giant cobra.

Looking up at the power-hungry Jafar, Aladdin got an idea. "The Genie has more power than you'll ever have!" he jeered.

"Yes-s-s-s," hissed Jafar. "You're right. I'm ready to make my third wish. I wish to be a genie."

The moment Jafar turned into a genie, Aladdin smiled. Jafar had forgotten that a genie must live in a lamp. In an instant, he and Iago disappeared inside their own magic lamp. They were gone for good!

The Sultan was overjoyed. That very day he changed
the law so that Jasmine could marry any man she chose.
And she chose Aladdin!

And what did Aladdin do with his third wish? He
kept his promise and wished for the Genie's freedom.

"Look out, world!" exclaimed the Genie. "Here I
come. I'm free!"